THOMAS & FRIENDS™

Race to the Rescue

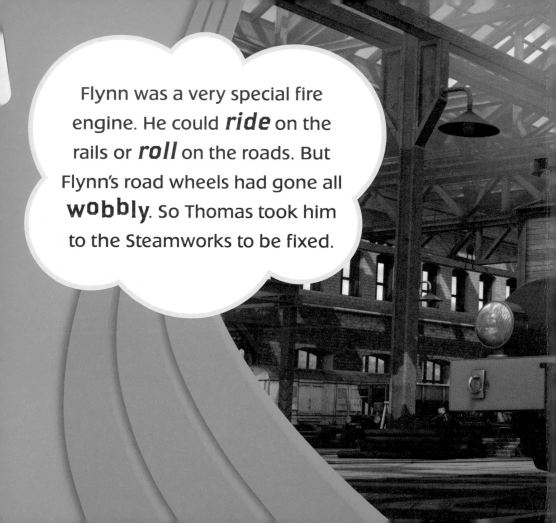

Flynn was a very special fire engine. He could *ride* on the rails or *roll* on the roads. But Flynn's road wheels had gone all **wobbly**. So Thomas took him to the Steamworks to be fixed.

Flynn was worried.
"Maybe my wheels will always **wobble!**" he said.

"No, they won't!" Thomas laughed, to make his friend feel better.

But Flynn was still worried, even after Victor had finished fixing his wheels.

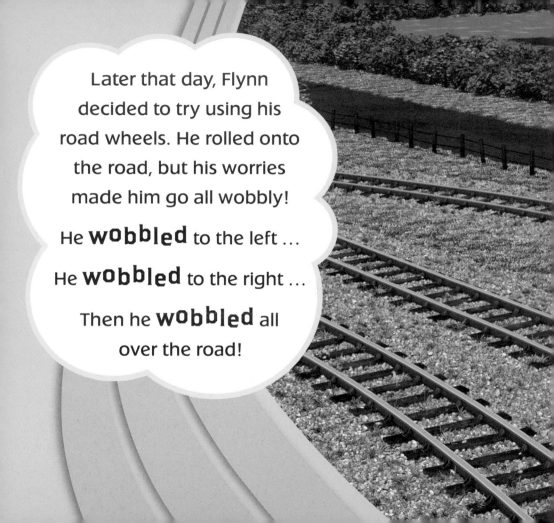

Later that day, Flynn decided to try using his road wheels. He rolled onto the road, but his worries made him go all wobbly!

He **wobbled** to the left …

He **wobbled** to the right …

Then he **wobbled** all over the road!

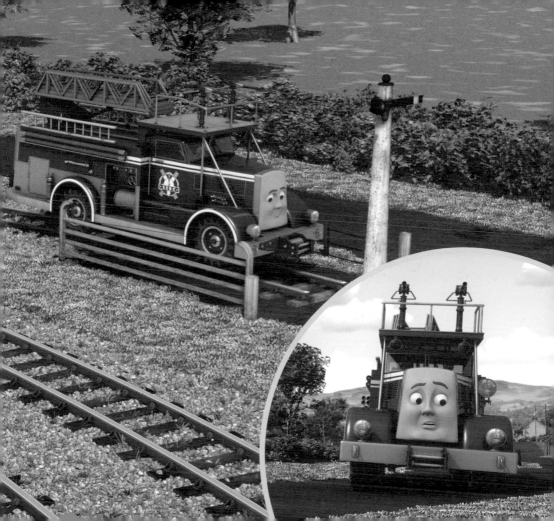

Just then, Charlie chuffed by.
"What's the matter, Flynn?"
he laughed. "You look like
a **Big Red Wobble**
on wheels!"

That made Flynn feel very
silly indeed.

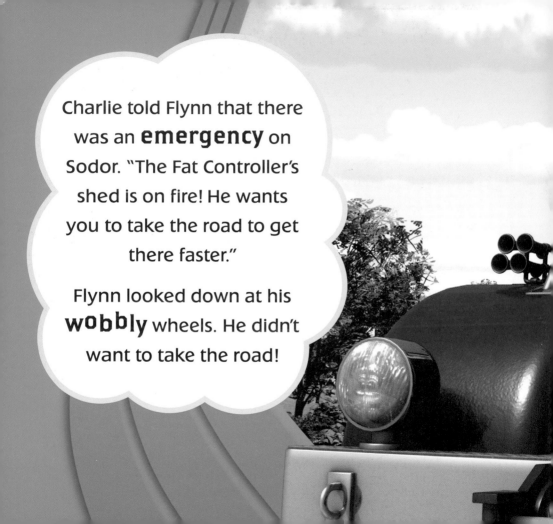

Charlie told Flynn that there was an **emergency** on Sodor. "The Fat Controller's shed is on fire! He wants you to take the road to get there faster."

Flynn looked down at his **wobbly** wheels. He didn't want to take the road!

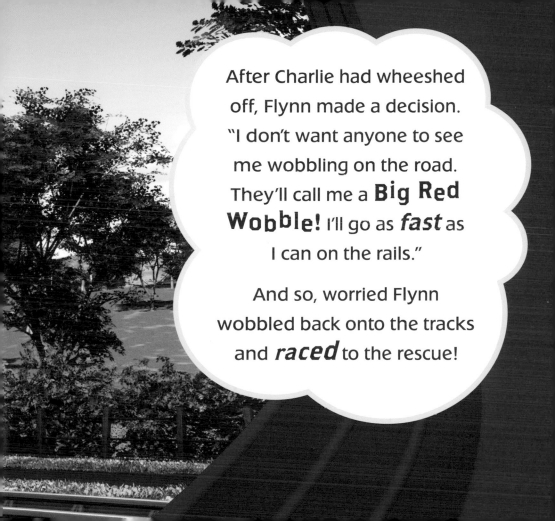

After Charlie had wheeshed off, Flynn made a decision. "I don't want anyone to see me wobbling on the road. They'll call me a **Big Red Wobble!** I'll go as *fast* as I can on the rails."

And so, worried Flynn wobbled back onto the tracks and *raced* to the rescue!

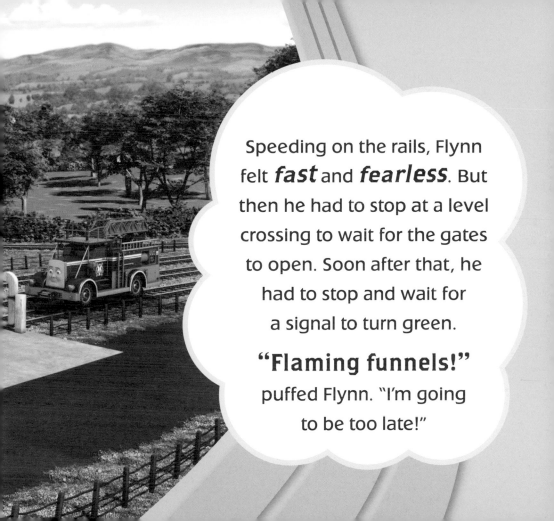

Speeding on the rails, Flynn felt *fast* and *fearless*. But then he had to stop at a level crossing to wait for the gates to open. Soon after that, he had to stop and wait for a signal to turn green.

"Flaming funnels!" puffed Flynn. "I'm going to be too late!"

When Flynn finally arrived at the shed, The Fat Controller was cross. "You were told to take the road!" he said. **"Hurry, Flynn!"**

Flynn looked at the crowd of people around him. To reach the fire, he had to go onto the road. But he was too worried about being called a **Big Red Wobble!**

Then a child shouted, "Hooray for Flynn!"

"He's Sodor's **hero!**" said another.

The crowd cheered for Flynn, making him feel very **brave** instead of worried. "I don't mind if they call me a Big Red Wobble. It's **Fiery Flynn** to the rescue!" he said.

Flynn **raced** onto the road and sped to the shed. With his strong water jets, he doused the flames until they flickered and fizzled. Flynn had put the fire out!

"**Well done, Flynn!**" said The Fat Controller. "I'm glad your wobble has gone."

Flynn was surprised to see he was right! "I'm not a Big Red Wobble any more," Flynn said proudly.

"No, you are Sodor's **Big Red Hero!**" said The Fat Controller. And that made Flynn's wheels wobble again … with **joy!**

PEEP! PEEP!

The End